Sadie Learns A Lesson

Written and Illustrated by

Jane Mathews

Published by Storytellers Ink
Seattle, Washington

ISBN 1-880812-18-5

Printed in Mexico

Respectfully dedicated to
Cleveland Amory and Polar Bear

Sadie is a house cat.

Tommie is a stray cat.

House cats are safe
from cars and trucks.

Honk
Honk

And unfriendly dogs
like Dindy.

And tough stray cats
like Tommie.

House cats have lots of
friends like Sadie's Kathleen.

KITTY LITTER
SADIE

Stray cats are often
lonely without friends.

HISS
HISS

All the same, Sadie spent much time thinking about how to escape outside.

One evening Kathleen
left the door open going
outside to get her bicycle.

747

Sadie noticed this right away. In no time she had sneaked out and was gone.

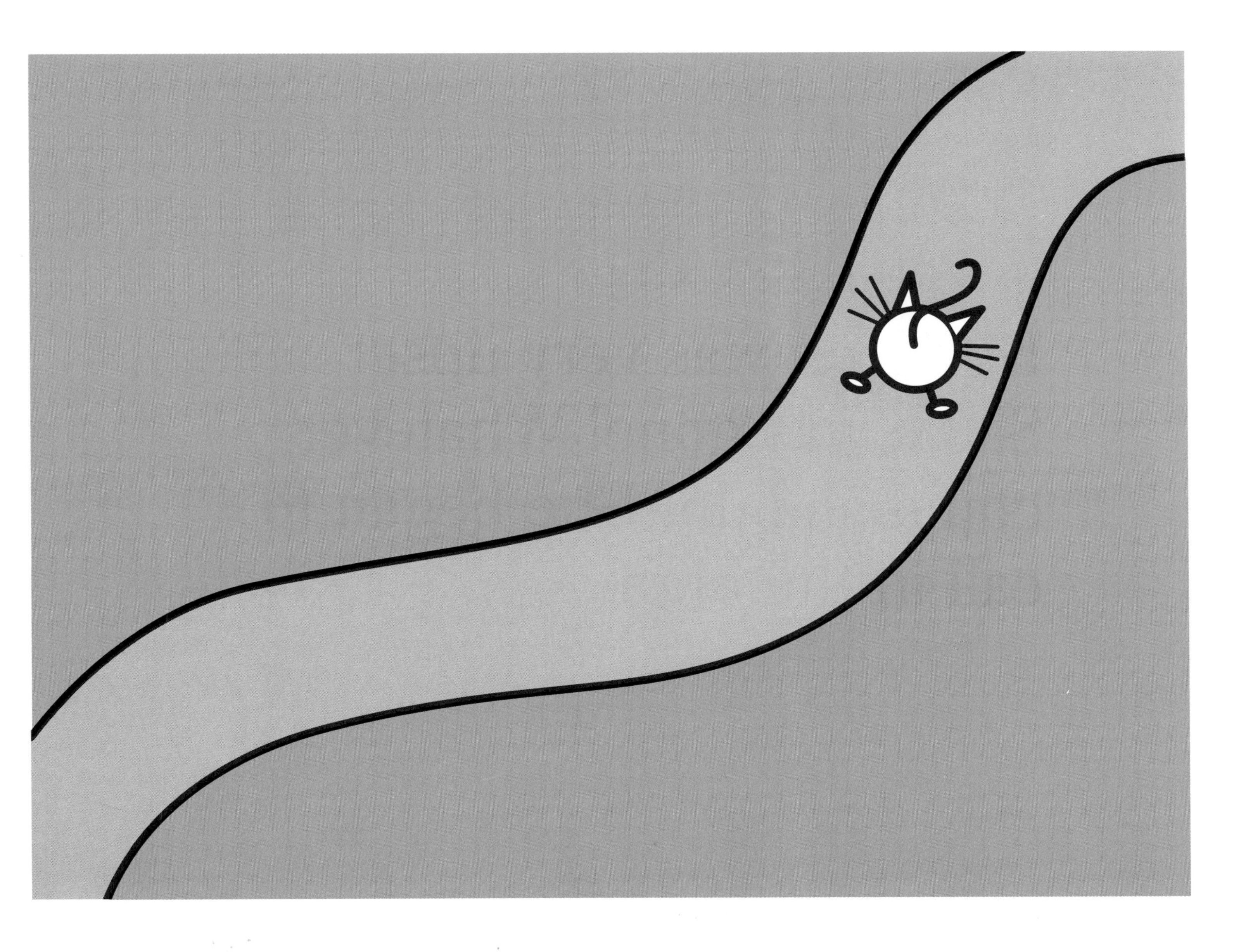

Kathleen was very upset
Sadie was gone! Whatever
could she do? She began to
call in the night.

747
Sāydēē

Soon, Sadie came running
by with Tommie the cat
and Dindy the dog
chasing her.

The truck had to screech to a stop to avoid running over Sadie.

Screech!

Dindy chased Sadie up a tree. Tommie escaped down the sewer.

When Dindy went home,
so did Sadie. Poor Tommie
didn't have any place to go.

Most certainly Sadie had learned her lesson. She decided she would remain a house cat forever.

PRRRR

Other "Light Up the Mind of a Child" books from Storytellers Ink

Kitty the Raccoon

The Living Mountain

Father Goose and His Goslings

The Butterfly Garden

Cousin Charlie the Crow

A Home for Ernie

Sandy of Laguna

I Thought I Heard a Tiger Roar

Tweak and the Absolutely Right Whale

J.G. Cougar's Great Adventure

Little Annie of Christian Creek

Sully the Seal and Alley the Cat

The Blue Kangaroo at the Zoo

Not for Sadie

Jonathan Jasper Jeremy Jones

The Blue Kangaroo

The Lost and Found Puppy

If a Seahorse Wore a Saddle

William's Story

Beautiful Joe

Black Beauty

Lobo the Wolf

Redruff the Partridge of the Don Valley

A Bug C

Bustop the Cat

The Adventures of Pilaf, Almondine and Tetrazini

Firefly Joe